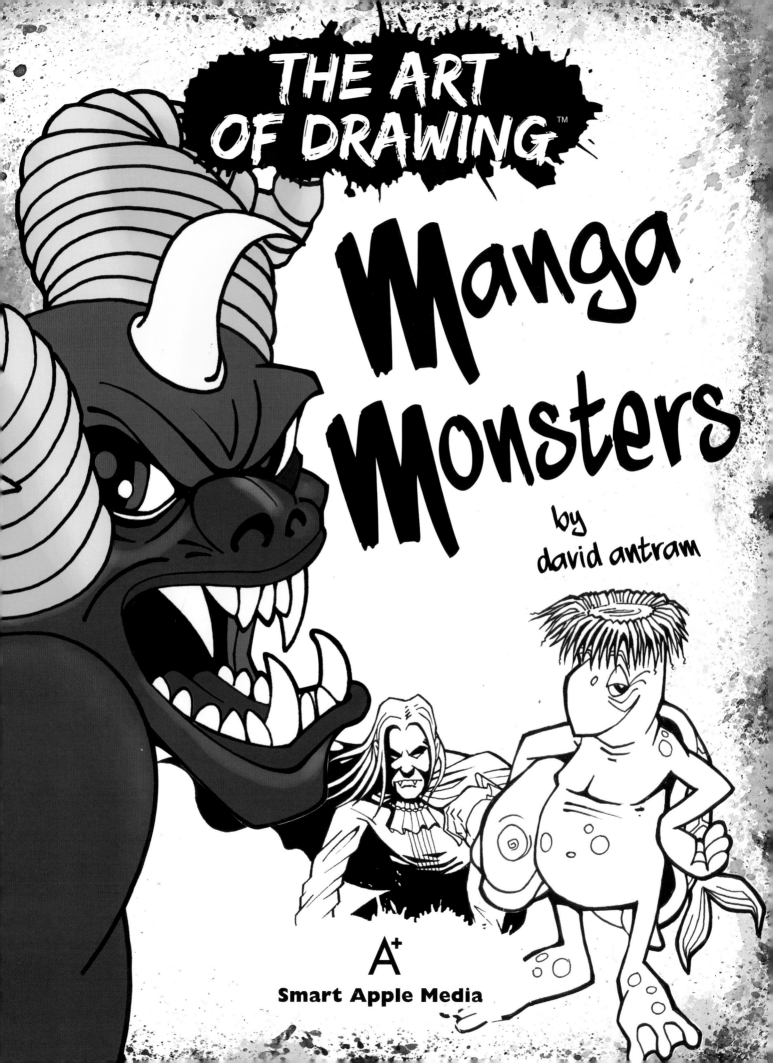

Published by Smart Apple Media,
an imprint of Black Rabbit Books
P.O. Box 3263, Mankato, Minnesota 56002
www.blackrabbitbooks.com

Published by arrangement with
The Salariya Book Company Ltd

Cataloging-in-Publication Data is available
from the Library of Congress

Printed in the United States
At Corporate Graphics,
North Mankato, Minnesota

9 8 7 6 5 4 3 2 1

ISBN: 978-1-62588-352-0

contents

4 making a start

6 perspective

8 materials

10 styles

12 body proportions

13 inking

14 heads

16 creases and folds

18 night hunter

20 witch

22 dragon slayer

24 akuma

26 kappa

28 ningyo

30 warrior girl

32 glossary and index

making a start

The key to drawing well is learning to look carefully. Study your subject until you know it really well. Keep a sketchbook with you and draw whenever you get the chance. Even doodling is good—it helps to make your drawing more confident. You'll soon develop your own style of drawing, but this book will help you to find your way.

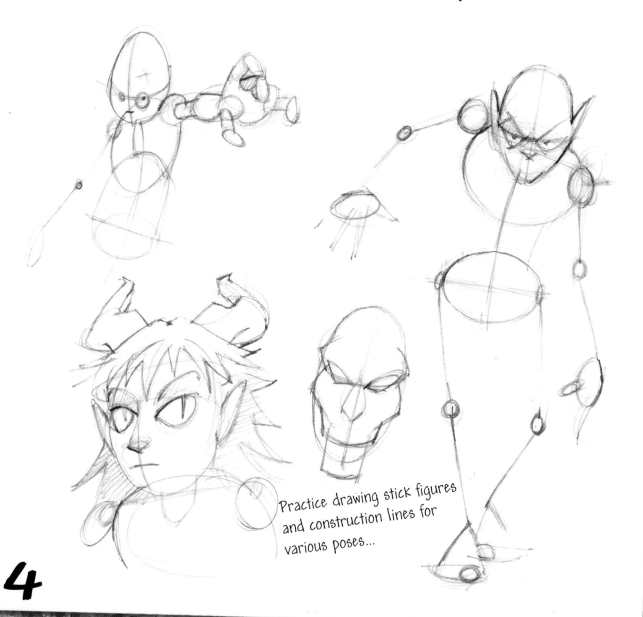

Practice drawing stick figures and construction lines for various poses...

quick sketches

Make quick sketches of the types of monsters you want to draw!

5

perspective

Perspective is a way of drawing objects so that they look as though they have three dimensions. Note how the part that is closest to you looks larger, and the part furthest away from you looks smaller. That's just how things look in real life.

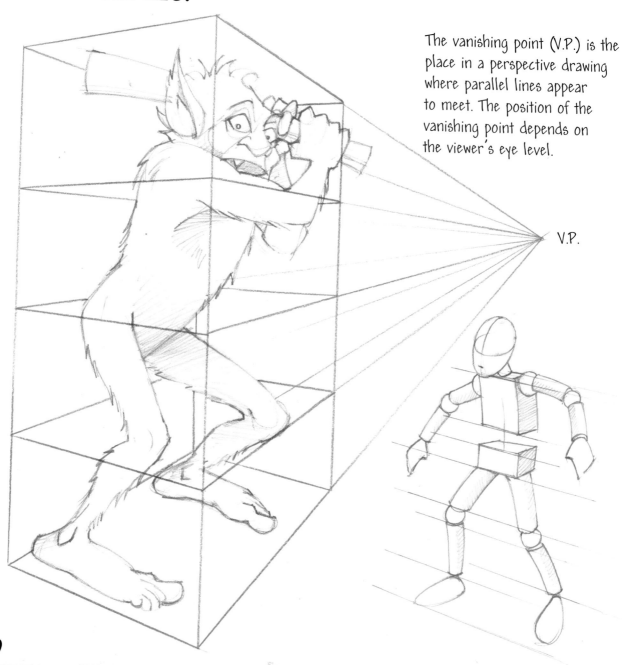

The vanishing point (V.P.) is the place in a perspective drawing where parallel lines appear to meet. The position of the vanishing point depends on the viewer's eye level.

V.P.

Two-point perspective uses two vanishing points: one for lines running along the length of the subject, and one on the opposite side for lines running across the width of the subject.

In this drawing the vanishing points are very low. This gives the impression that you are looking up at the figure—very dramatic!

V.P.

V.P.

Low eye level
(view from below)

V.P.

V.P.

High eye level
(view from above)

V.P.

V.P. = vanishing point

Three-point perspective adds a third vanishing point above or below the drawing (above right.)

V.P.

V.P.

7

materials

Remember, the best equipment and materials will not necessarily make the best drawing—only practice will.

pencils

Try out different grades of pencils. Hard pencils make fine gray lines and soft pencils make softer, darker marks.

erasers

are useful for cleaning up drawings and removing construction lines.

paper

Bristol paper is good for crayons, pastels, and felt-tip pens. Watercolor paper is thicker; it is the best choice for water-based paints or inks.

Use this sandpaper block if you want to shape your pencil to a really sharp point.

inks

Use colored inks straight from the bottle or dilute them with water.

felt-tip pens

Felt-tips usually come in sets of mixed colors. The ones that make very thin lines are called fineliners.

Ink

Mixing palette

Fineliners

Dip-in pen nibs

Brushes

Correction fluid

Gouache

pens

Technical drawing pens have cartridges which can be refilled or replaced. Old-fashioned dip-in pens are much cheaper and come in many different styles and sizes.

Watercolors

paints

Ordinary watercolors are translucent (see-through); gouache is not. Try other kinds of paints, too.

Technical drawing pens

9

styles

Try different types of drawing papers and materials. Experiment with pens, from felt-tips to ballpoints, and make interesting marks. What happens if you draw with pen and ink on wet paper?

Felt-tips come in a range of line widths. The wider pens are good for filling in large areas of flat tone.

Ink silhouette

Silhouette is a style of drawing which mainly relies on solid dark shapes.

Pencil drawings can include a vast amount of detail and tone. Try different grades of pencil to get a range of light and shade effects in your drawings.

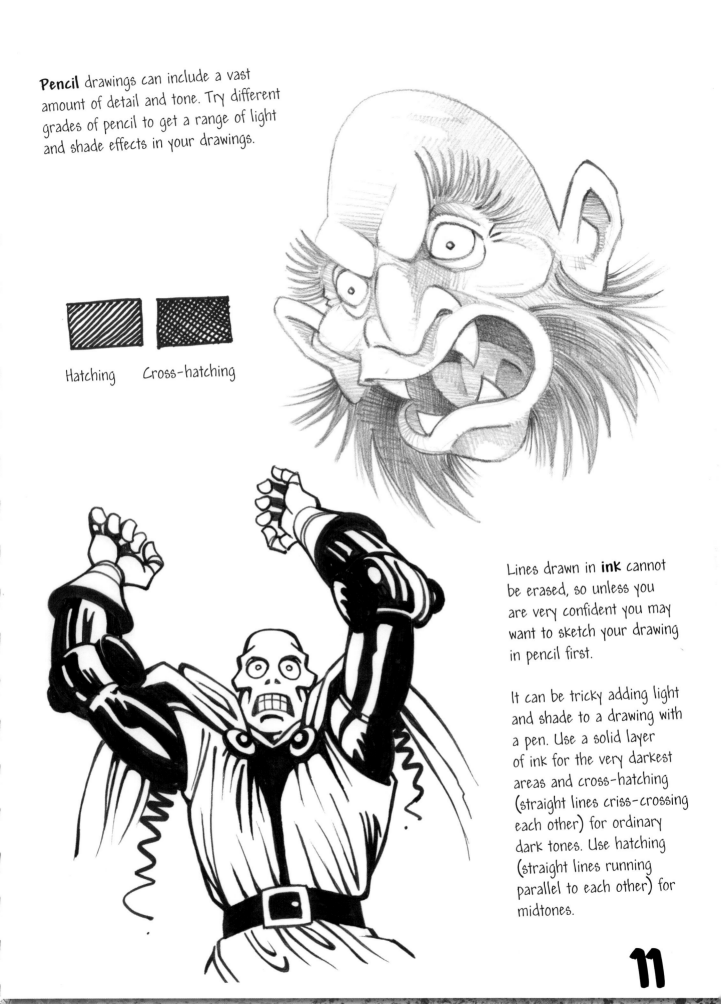

Hatching   Cross-hatching

Lines drawn in **ink** cannot be erased, so unless you are very confident you may want to sketch your drawing in pencil first.

It can be tricky adding light and shade to a drawing with a pen. Use a solid layer of ink for the very darkest areas and cross-hatching (straight lines criss-crossing each other) for ordinary dark tones. Use hatching (straight lines running parallel to each other) for midtones.

11

body proportions

Heads in manga are drawn slightly bigger than in real life. Legs and hips make up more than half the overall height of the figure.

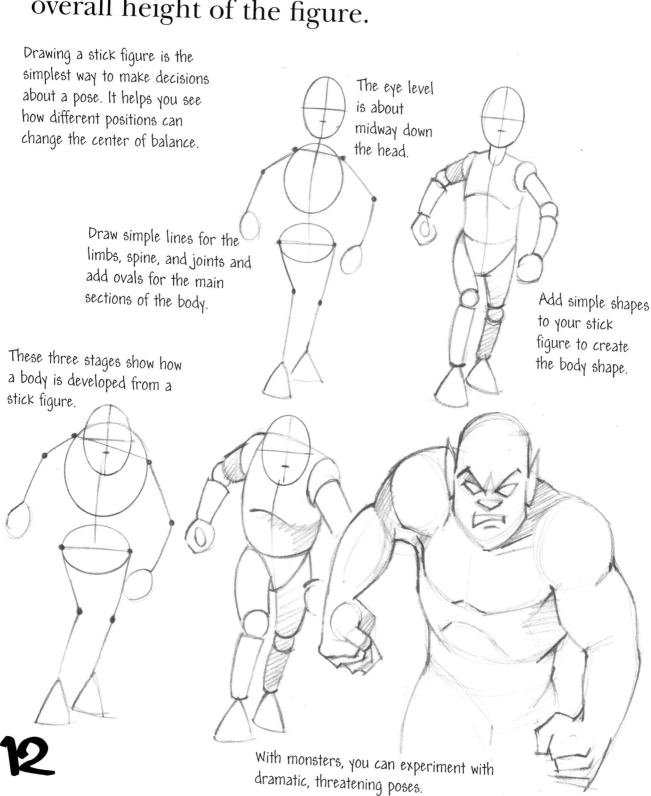

Drawing a stick figure is the simplest way to make decisions about a pose. It helps you see how different positions can change the center of balance.

The eye level is about midway down the head.

Draw simple lines for the limbs, spine, and joints and add ovals for the main sections of the body.

Add simple shapes to your stick figure to create the body shape.

These three stages show how a body is developed from a stick figure.

With monsters, you can experiment with dramatic, threatening poses.

inking

Here's one way of inking over your final pencil drawing.

Refillable inking pens come in various tip sizes. The tip is what determines the width of the line that is drawn. Sizes include: 0.1, 0.5, 1.0, 2.0 mm.

Different tones of ink can be used to add depth to the drawing.
Mix ink with water to achieve the tones you need.

heads

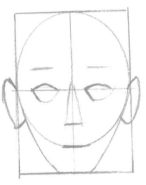

Manga heads have a distinctive style and shape. Manga monsters, specifically, may have exaggerated features such as noses, ears, and teeth.

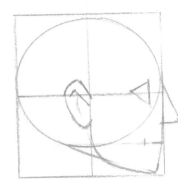

1. Start by drawing a square. Fit the head, chin, and ear inside it to keep the correct proportions.

2. Draw construction lines to position the top of the ear and the base of the nose.

Practice drawing heads from different angles...

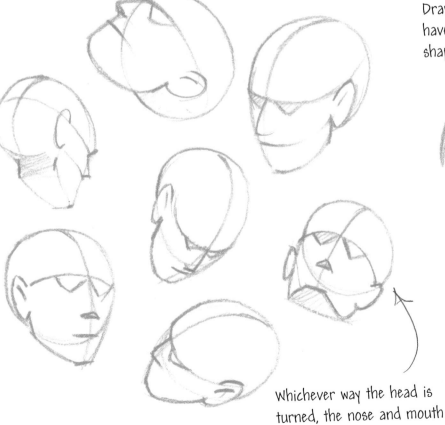

Drawing a profile view means you can have more fun with monster head shapes, noses, mouths, ears, and hair!

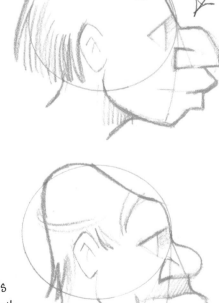

Whichever way the head is turned, the nose and mouth always stay on the center line.

14

M

onsters can have all sorts of weird and wonderful heads. See what strange heads you can imagine.

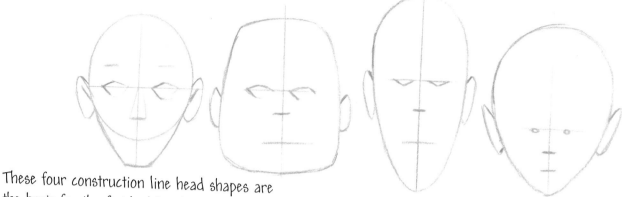

These four construction line head shapes are the basis for the finished heads below.

Frustrated

Plotting

Sinister

Very angry!

creases and folds

Clothes fall into natural creases and folds when worn. Look at real people to see how fabric drapes and how it falls into creases. This will help you to dress your characters more realistically.

Creases occur where excess fabric gathers in folds. You will need to learn how and where to draw creases, as you will need to add them to your character's clothes to make your pictures lifelike. Try draping fabric over everyday objects and sketching what you see.

Drawing from life can help you understand where and why creases and folds occur.

The way fabric is drawn can instantly give a sense of movement and action to a pose.

The way fabric hangs depends on the type and weight of the material.

Fabric can flow or fold with movement or weight.

The weight of the fabric is making it sag.

The fabric here curves with movement.

night hunter

The night hunter is a vampire. He is moody, and very dangerous to cross. Beware of dark shadows where you won't see him coming!

1. Draw ovals for the head, body, and hips. Add center lines to divide the head vertically and horizontally. These will help you to place the ears and the nose.

2. Add lines for the spine and the angle of the hips and shoulders.

3. Draw stick arms and legs, with dots where the joints are. Add outline shapes for hands and feet.

These little circles are to remind you where the elbows and knees go.

A flowing cape gives the character a dramatic edge.

4. Using the construction lines as a guide, start to build up the main shapes and features.

20

Add a sharp hairline. Longer hair creates a wild effect.

5. Flesh out the main body parts, add hair, and draw a little more detail on the face.

6. If you don't want your construction lines to show, erase them before you do the final shading and details.

7. Now finish all the little details such as the facial expression, the clothes (remember folds and creases!), and shading. Shade everywhere the light would not reach.

Look at pictures of vampires to get a feel for the type of clothing they might wear.

Why not try finishing this drawing off in ink? Ink will highlight the dark shadows and the harsh features of the vampire's face and costume.

witch

The witch is very old and can see into the future. She can tell you your fortune but always at a price. She doesn't like children.

1. Draw a circle for the head and ovals for the body and hips.

2. Add lines for the spine and the angle of the hips and shoulders.

4. Use your guidelines to sketch in the neck and facial features.

3. Draw stick arms and legs with dots for the joints.

Small circles indicate the positions of elbows and knees.

5. Using the construction lines as a guide, start drawing in the main shapes of the body. Pencil in details such as the cape and walking stick.

20

6. Now start to sketch out the final shapes of clothes, hair, arms, and legs. Think about what kind of facial expression the witch would have.

Draw in the shape of the fingers.

7. If you don't want your construction lines to show, erase them carefully before you add the finishing touches: shading, facial features, folds and creases on the clothes.

Long, bony fingers

Add creases to the cloth.

Try going over the main outlines in ink for a different outcome. Erase any pencil drawing underneath.

21

the art of drawing
dragon slayer

The dragon slayer is a fierce and ferocious knight. He'll stop at nothing on his quest to fight and kill every dragon in the land.

1. Draw ovals for the head and hips and a circle for the body.

2. Add lines for the spine and the angle of the hips and shoulders.

3. Add a line for the sword.

4. Draw stick arms and legs with dots for the joints.

5. Using your construction lines, add the neck and sketch in the facial features.

Draw two circles and a construction line for the dragon's head, too. Add more detail as you go along.

6. Flesh out the arms and legs, using circles to indicate elbows and knees.

22

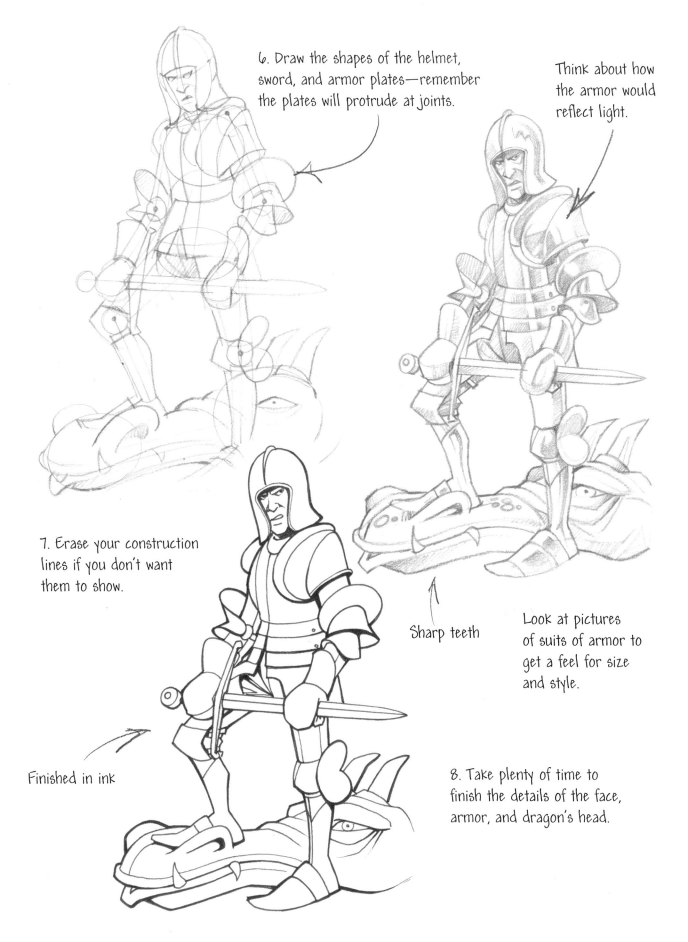

6. Draw the shapes of the helmet, sword, and armor plates—remember the plates will protrude at joints.

Think about how the armor would reflect light.

7. Erase your construction lines if you don't want them to show.

Sharp teeth

Look at pictures of suits of armor to get a feel for size and style.

Finished in ink

8. Take plenty of time to finish the details of the face, armor, and dragon's head.

akuma

Akuma is Japanese for "devil," a demon who haunts dreams. If a person is bad, the akuma poses riddles to decide his or her fate.

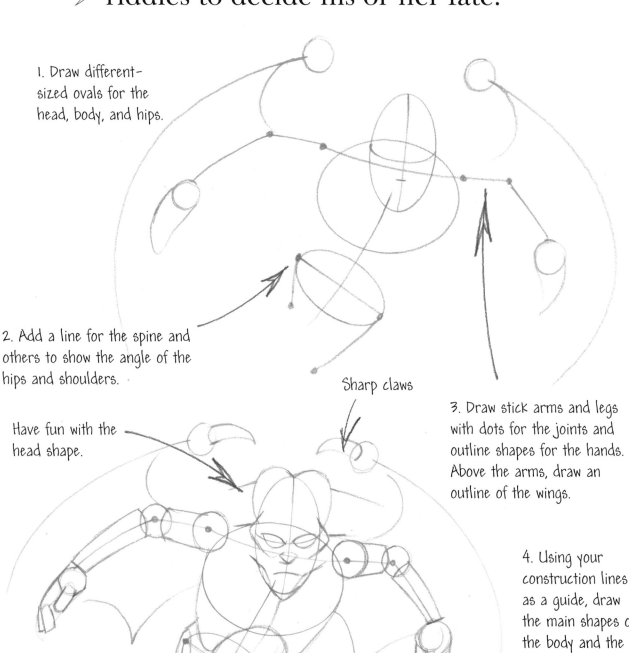

1. Draw different-sized ovals for the head, body, and hips.

2. Add a line for the spine and others to show the angle of the hips and shoulders.

Have fun with the head shape.

Sharp claws

3. Draw stick arms and legs with dots for the joints and outline shapes for the hands. Above the arms, draw an outline of the wings.

4. Using your construction lines as a guide, draw the main shapes of the body and the positions of the facial features.

Circles with dots show the position of the joints.

24

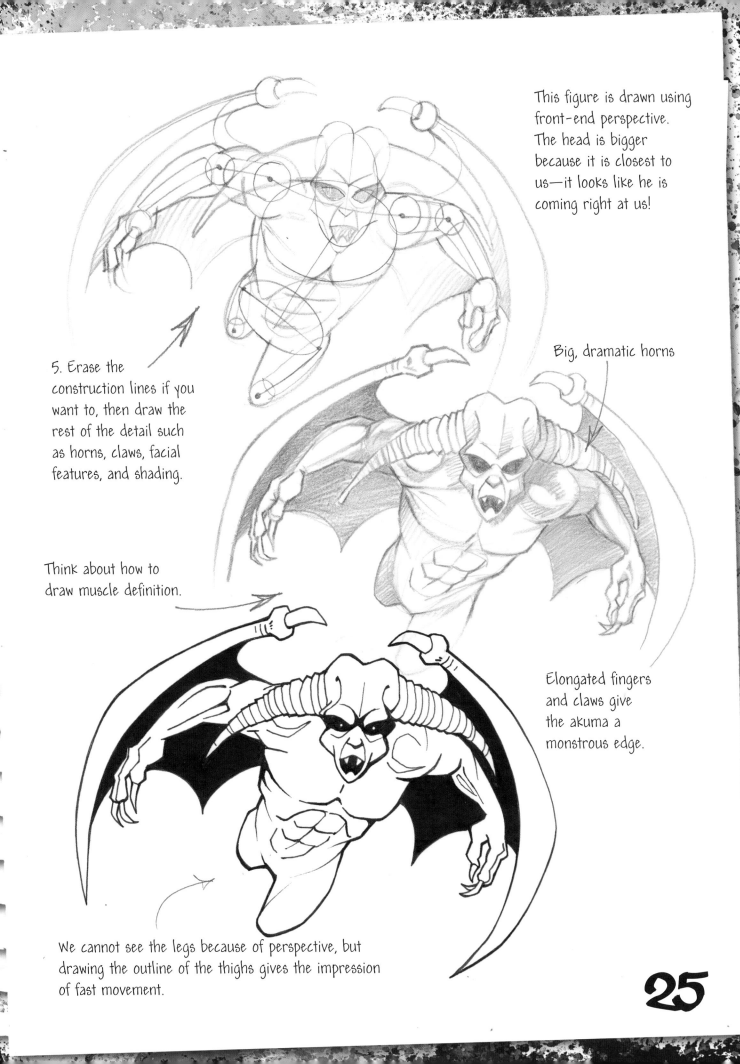

This figure is drawn using front-end perspective. The head is bigger because it is closest to us—it looks like he is coming right at us!

5. Erase the construction lines if you want to, then draw the rest of the detail such as horns, claws, facial features, and shading.

Big, dramatic horns

Think about how to draw muscle definition.

Elongated fingers and claws give the akuma a monstrous edge.

We cannot see the legs because of perspective, but drawing the outline of the thighs gives the impression of fast movement.

25

kappa

The kappa is a water demon. He is hundreds of years old, and he kills fish and other sea creatures. He is sly, and it is considered bad luck if you see him.

1. As you've done before, draw ovals for the head and body and a big circle for the hips, as the kappa is quite a round creature.

Add the hat shape.

3. Draw stick arms and legs, with dots for the joints.

4. Using construction lines, flesh out the main parts of the body and face. Draw the basic shapes of the fish head and tail.

2. Draw construction lines for the spine and the angle of the hips and shoulders.

Webbed hands and feet!

26

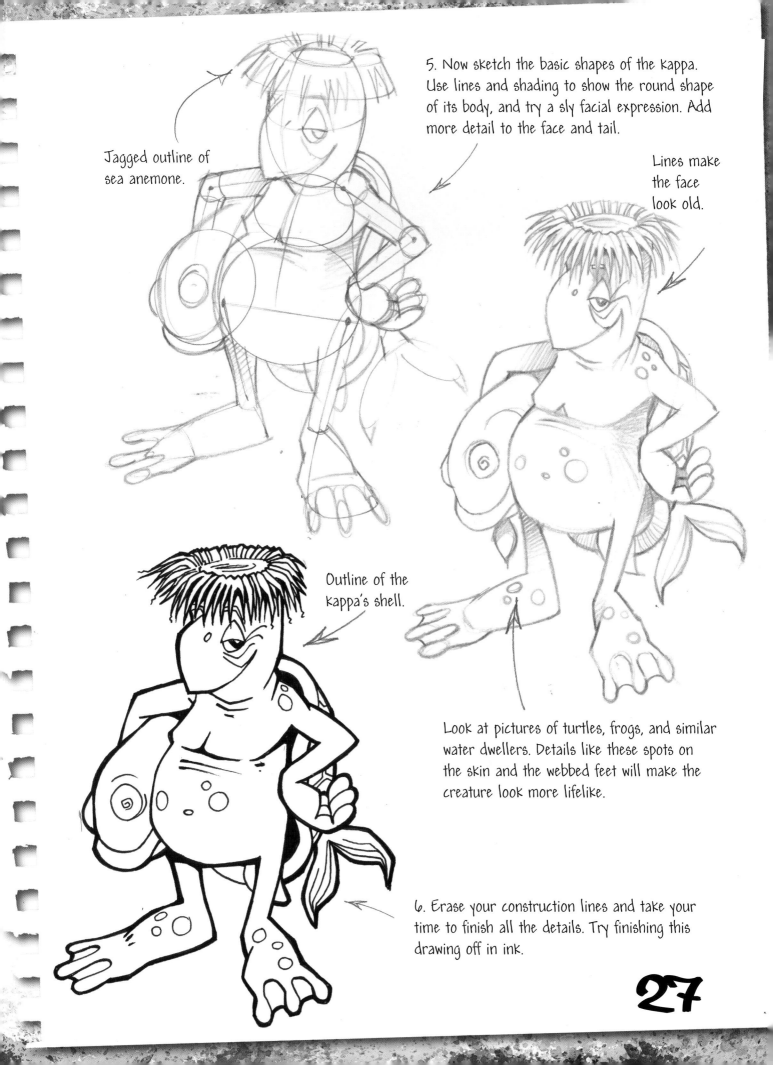

Jagged outline of sea anemone.

5. Now sketch the basic shapes of the kappa. Use lines and shading to show the round shape of its body, and try a sly facial expression. Add more detail to the face and tail.

Lines make the face look old.

Outline of the kappa's shell.

Look at pictures of turtles, frogs, and similar water dwellers. Details like these spots on the skin and the webbed feet will make the creature look more lifelike.

6. Erase your construction lines and take your time to finish all the details. Try finishing this drawing off in ink.

27

ningyo

The ningyo is a very beautiful mermaid, but also very dangerous. She rules the sea and lures sailors to their death.

1. Draw the various ovals and construction lines as you have done before. This time, instead of stick legs, draw a basic line and fish tail shape.

2. Using your construction lines, add the basic shapes of the torso, arms, and tail. Sketch in the facial features.

Start drawing wisps of hair and build this up gradually to get a swept mane effect.

Don't forget the webbed hands!

28

Dramatic facial expression

3. Start drawing the details, such as the facial expression and the mermaid's clothes. Keep building up the hair too!

Think about the kind of outfit this mermaid would wear. It should be feminine.

Add line detail on the tail.

4. Erase construction lines before finishing off all the details.

5. Here's the same drawing finished with brush and ink. Decide which lines you want to ink in before you make any brush marks.

29

warrior girl

The warrior girl is warlike and ruthless. She protects her village fearlessly, and any trespassers fall victim to her wrath.

1. Draw the basic ovals and construction lines as usual. Remember the lines for the spine and hips. Draw stick arms and legs with dots for the joints. Draw a line for the scepter too.

2. Sketch the arms and legs and the main facial features. Think about the pose of the warrior girl—she is putting her weight on her right leg, so her body is leaning slightly left.

Circles represent the joints.

Practice drawing clenched hands to get an idea of grip.

30

3. Draw the details of the clothes, face, hands, and feet. Gradually build up the hair.

Look at pictures of skulls and practice sketching them.

Draw these tufts in the same way as the hair.

4. There is a lot of detail in this drawing, such as the fringes on the clothing, the jewelry, and the scepter.

Knee pads

5. Erase the construction lines and try finishing this drawing in ink.

Sharp claws

31

glossary

Composition The positioning of the various parts of a picture on the drawing paper.

Construction lines Guidelines used in the early stages of a drawing which are usually erased later.

Cross-hatching A series of criss-crossing lines used to add shade to a drawing.

Hatching A series of parallel lines used to add shade to a drawing.

Manga A Japanese word for "comic" or "cartoon"; also the style of drawing that is used in Japanese comics.

Neko The Japanese word for "cat"; also a manga character that is part-human, part-cat.

Silhouette A drawing that shows only a dark shape, like a shadow, sometimes with a few details left white.

Three-dimensional Having an effect of depth, so as to look like a real character rather than a flat picture.

Tone The contrast between light and shade that helps to add depth to a picture.

Vanishing point The place in a perspective drawing where parallel lines appear to meet.

index

A
akuma 24–25

C
claws 24–25, 31
construction lines 4, 8, 14–15, 18–31
correction fluid 9, 13
cross-hatching 11

D
dragon slayer 22–23

E
erasers 8
eye level 6–7

F
facial expressions 15
felt-tip pens 9
folds and creases 16–17,

G
gouache 9

H
hair 14, 19, 21, 28–29, 31
hatching 11
heads 14–15

I
ink 8–11, 13, 19, 21, 23

K
kappa 26–27

L
legs 20

N
night hunter 18–19
ningyo 28–29

P
paper 8
pencils 8, 11
pens 9, 10
perspective 6–7, 25
proportions 12, 14

S
sandpaper block 8
shading, shadows 11, 19, 21, 25, 27
silhouette 10
sketching 5–6
stick figures 4, 12

V
vanishing points 6–7

W
warrior girl 30–31
watercolor 9
witch 20–21